MY 1ST GRAPHIC NOVEL®

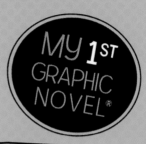

Tide Pool Trouble

MY FIRST GRAPHIC NOVELS ARE PUBLISHED BY STONE ARCH BOOKS
A CAPSTONE IMPRINT
151 GOOD COUNSEL DRIVE, P.O. BOX 669
MANKATO, MINNESOTA 56002
WWW.CAPSTONEPUB.COM

Library of Congress Cataloging-in-Publication data is available on the
Library of Congress website.

ISBN: 978-1-4342-2517-7 (library binding)
ISBN: 978-1-4342-3059-1 (paperback)

Summary: Mason and his cousin are going to the beach. But when his aunt takes them
to a tide pool, Mason is disappointed. Will Mason learn to enjoy the tide pool like he enjoys
the regular beach?

Art Director: **KAY FRASER**
Graphic Designer: **HILARY WACHOLZ**
Production Specialist: **MICHELLE BIEDSCHEID**

Photo Credits: iStockphoto Inc.: Alex Lui, 28, (top left); Dushenina, 24 (bottom); Goluba, 28 (top
right); Hanis, 20 (top); javarman, 28 (bottom left); SPrada, 17, 18, backcover; Shutterstock: Alta
Oosthuizen, 9, 23; Charmaine A Harvey, 10, 12, 13 (bottom), 29; Iakov Kalinin, 6; jcpjr, 8; Joy M.
Prescott, cover, 22 (top), 24 (top); Michael Zysman, 13 (top); Nikonov, 19; Serg64, 14, 22 (bottom);
Strider, 7; Paul Clarke, 4, 5; Steve Harpster, 3, 17, 21; Undersea Discoveries, 28 (bottom right)

In memory of two wonderful boys, Dylan and Brendon Lord.
You are greatly missed. -M.L.

Printed in the United States of America in Stevens Point, Wisconsin.
092010
005934WZS11

Tide Pool Trouble

written by **Michelle Lord**   illustrated by **Steve Harpster**

STONE ARCH BOOKS
a capstone imprint

HOW TO READ A GRAPHIC NOVEL

Graphic novels are easy to read. Boxes called panels show you how to follow the story. Look at the panels from left to right and top to bottom.

Read the word boxes and word balloons from left to right as well. Don't forget the sound and action words in the pictures.

The pictures and the words work together to tell the whole story.

Every summer, Mason went to the same beach with his mom and dad.

He built sandcastles.

He wiggled his toes in the sand.

He floated on his rubber raft.

Today Mason was going to the beach with his cousin Lola. Their aunt Molly was taking them.

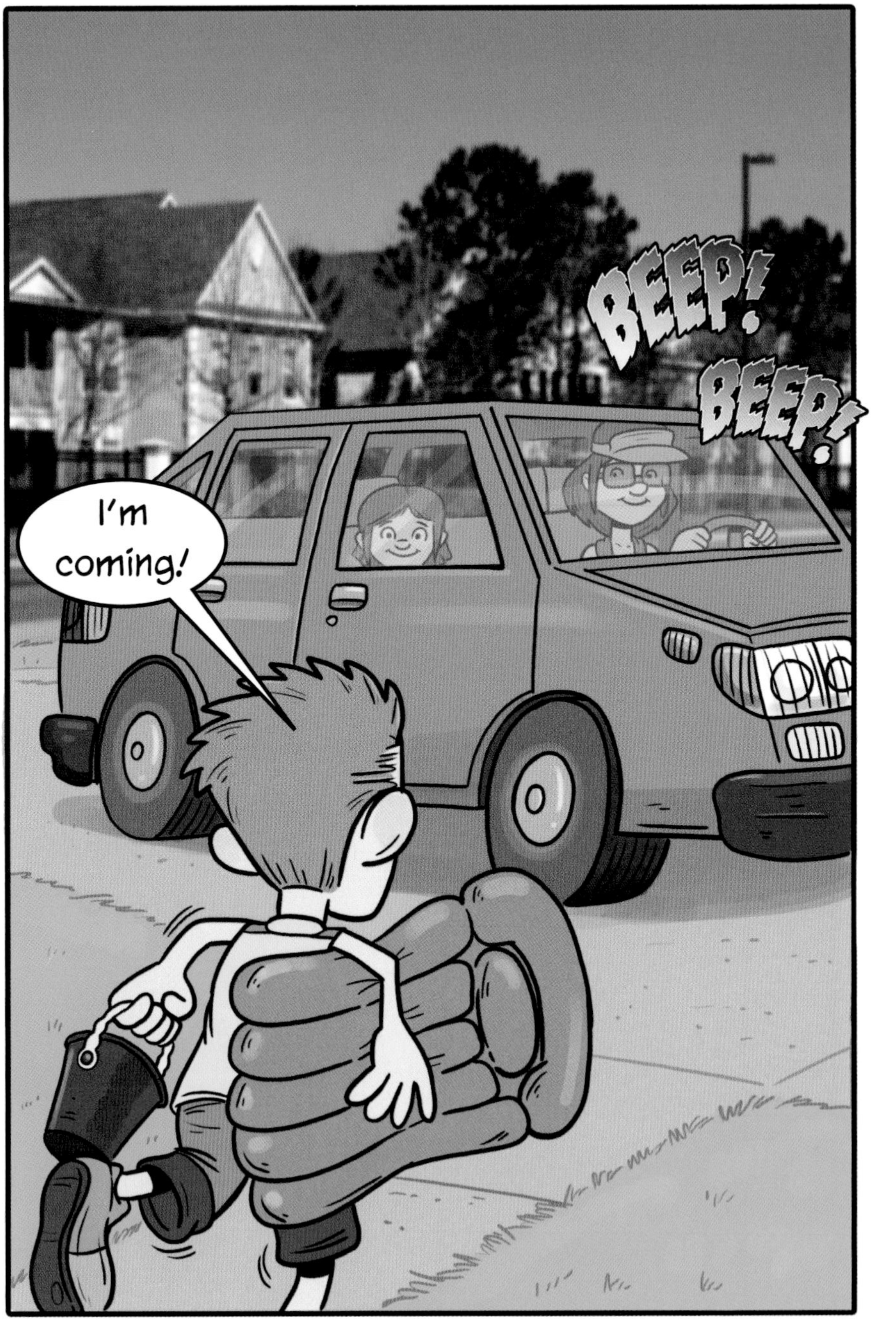
BEEP! BEEP!
I'm coming!

Molly drove and drove. She drove past the beach Mason liked.

Molly finally stopped the van. Mason and Lola jumped out.

This beach didn't have much sand. It didn't even have a place to swim.

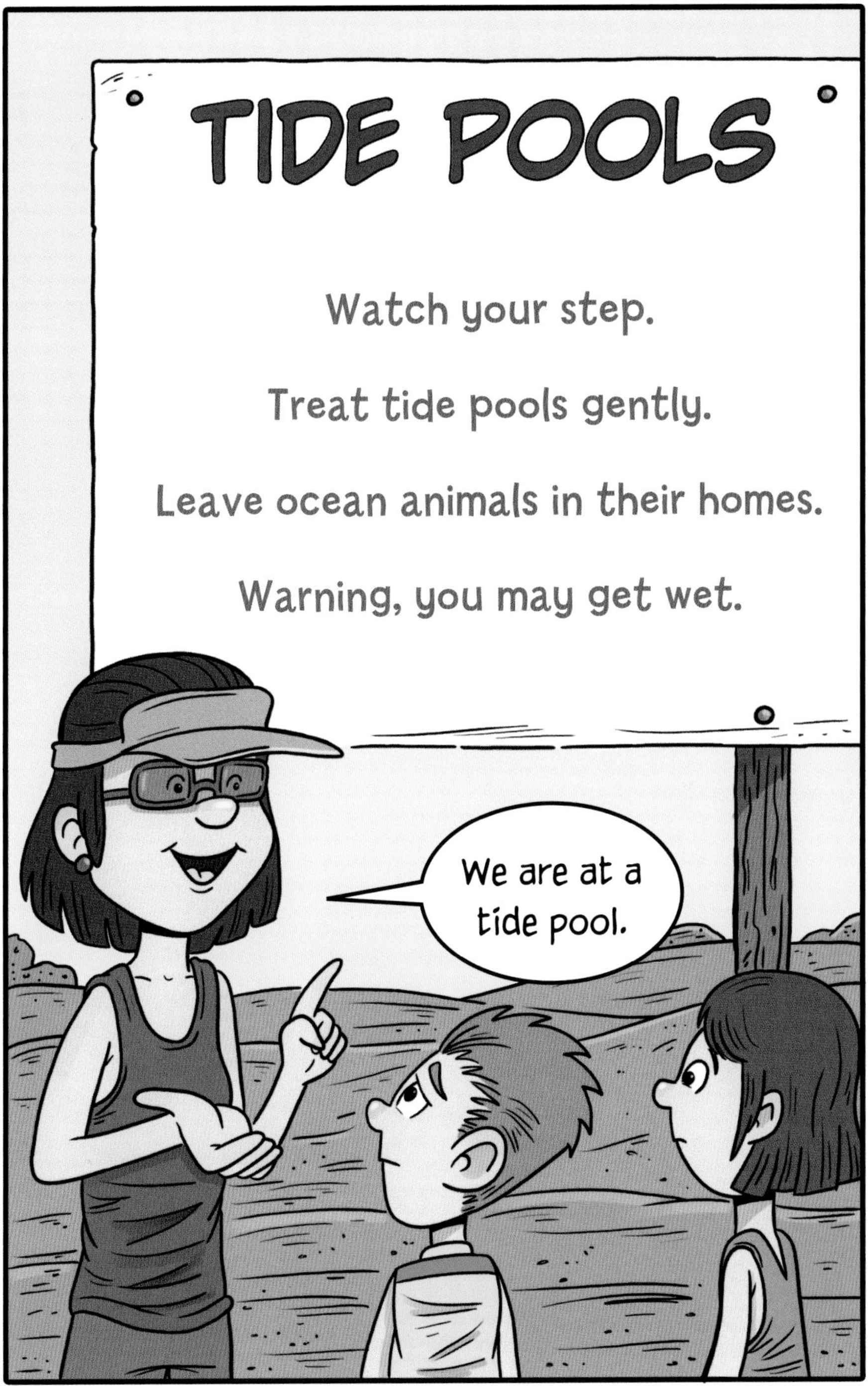
TIDE POOLS
Watch your step.
Treat tide pools gently.
Leave ocean animals in their homes.
Warning, you may get wet.
We are at a tide pool.

Molly told them a tide pool is a different type of beach.

The tide went in and out. The wind blew.

Mason almost slipped on the wet rocks.

Aunt Molly pointed to a pool of water. Mason and Lola bent down to look.

The tide pool was alive. It was filled with lots of different sea creatures.

Mason and Lola saw a sea lemon slither. They saw crabs scuttle. They saw starfish grip the rocks.

Mason forgot about his raft. He forgot about his pail and shovel.

Molly showed Mason how to touch the animals.

Mason dipped his fingers into the water.

The sea cucumber felt slimy.

The seaweed felt smooth.

The sea lemon felt soft.

A wave crashed onto the rocks.

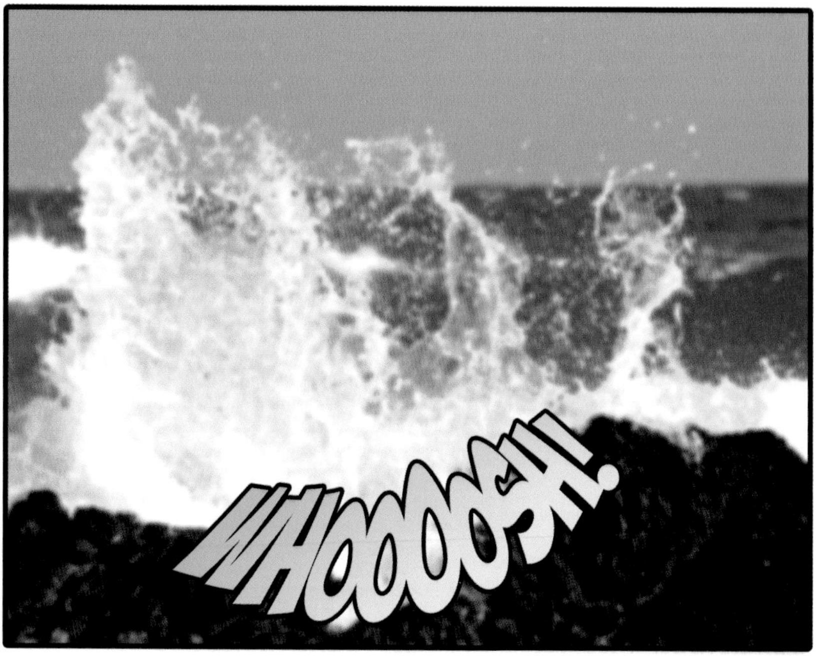
WHOOOOSH!

Mason and Lola held onto the rocks like the starfish did.

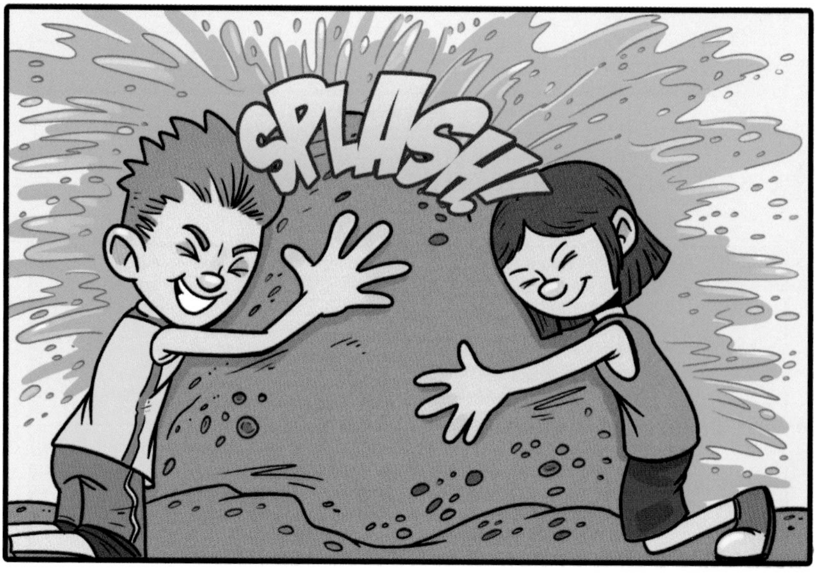
SPLASH!

Everyone was soaking wet!

21

The wave had washed a fish ashore.

Mason grabbed his bucket. He filled it with water.

Mason plopped the fish into the bucket.

He poured it into the ocean. The fish swam away.

Mason was wet and cold. He smelled like fish. But he didn't care.

Mason liked this new beach, even if it was a little different. And at the end of the day, everyone was happy and tired.

THE END

BIOGRAPHIES

MICHELLE LORD lives in New Braunfels, Texas, with her husband, her three children, her two labradoodles, and her one dachshund. This summer she visited tide pools on the Oregon Coast for the first time.

STEVE HARPSTER loved drawing funny cartoons, mean monsters, and goofy gadgets since he was able to pick up a pencil. Now he does it for a living. Steve lives in Columbus, Ohio, with his wonderful wife, Karen, and their sheepdog, Doodle.

GLOSSARY

RAFT (RAFT) — a rubber floating device

SEA CREATURES (SEE KREE-churz) — small animals that live in the water

SEA CUCUMBER (SEE KYOO-kuhm-bur) — a small sea creature that looks like a cucumber

SEA LEMON (SEE LEM-uhn) — a colorful sea slug

STARFISH (STAR-fish) — a sea animal shaped like a star with five or more arms

TIDE (TIDE) — the constant change of the sea level

TIDE POOL (TIDE POOL) — a pool of water left after the tide flows away from the shore and the water level is low again

Mason's Favorite Sea Creatures

At first, I was not excited about the new beach. But it was easy to get excited once I saw all the cool sea creatures in the tide pool. Look how cool they are!

Starfish

Sea Cucumber

Crab

Sea Lemon

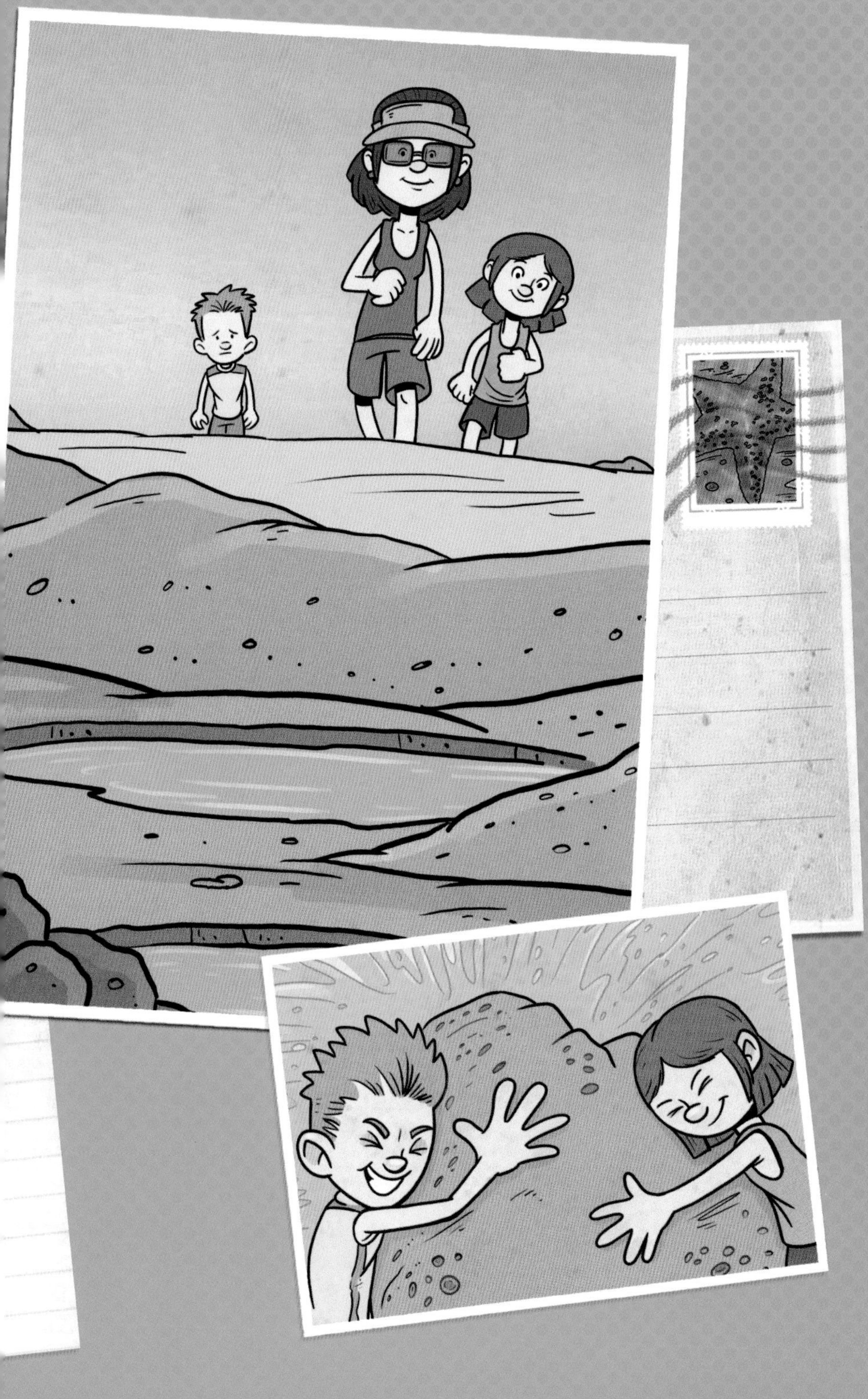

DISCUSSION QUESTIONS

1. Have you been to a beach or a tide pool? If so, did you like it? If not, would you want to go?

2. Mason was disappointed when he arrived at the beach. Why was he unhappy?

3. Mason changed his mind about the trip. What do you think made him enjoy it?

WRITING PROMPTS

1. Have you been on a trip that did not turn out the way you planned? Write about it.

2. Draw a picture of what you might find in a tide pool.

3. Can you think of another title for this story? Draw a new cover for this book and add your new title.

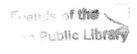